For Nikolai and Bruno

Ute Krause

Nick AND THE NASTY KNIGHT

NorthSouth
New York / London

Sir Nestor the Nasty was the meanest, rottenest, greediest knight you can imagine. So wicked was he that people would run and hide whenever he and his men rode through their village. So scary was he that babies cried just at the sight of his picture.

"Bring me your money!" Sir Nestor the Nasty bellowed, and woe betide anyone who came empty-handed. Those who did not pay were taken captive and forced to work from morn till night in the dark, dank bowels of the knight's castle.

This is why Nick came to be working for the knight—his mother owed Sir Nestor a lot of money, though Nick's family was very poor and the knight was so rich that even his toilet was made of pure gold. Why, the Nasty Knight barely used his own legs to walk anywhere. Instead, he had seven servants who carried him around.

Nick could only dream of such a comfortable life.
Instead, he had to get up before sunrise . . .

Mine

Mine

chop wood . . .   fetch fifty buckets
of water . . .
do the dishes . . .

Mine

and feed the pets; and
once he finished, he
started over again at
the beginning until he
fell into bed completely
exhausted by nightfall.
Every day was like this
without a single break.

Something really had
to change.

PETS

One night Nick decided that it was time to escape from the castle. When everyone was asleep, he snuck away armed with a rope and a bow and arrow. He had not gone far when suddenly he heard footsteps.

"The guards! I must hide—and fast!" Nick said to himself.
Quickly he slipped through the nearest door—into what he
thought was a closet. Just in time!

Nick took a look around his hiding place.
He had to pinch himself. This was no closet!
Instead, he had landed in the Nasty Knight's
treasure chamber! Piled high before him were
jewels and gems, silver and gold, treasures
from all over the world. They shone so
brightly that Nick had to close his eyes.

Suddenly he realized that the bright light did not actually come from the treasure. No, it came from a single gold coin that lay in the middle of the room. Just as Nick picked it up, he heard voices right outside the door.

THE GUARDS!

As fast as he could, he hurried to the window, tied his rope to an arrow, and shot it over to a tree on the opposite side of the moat. After he'd fastened his end of the rope to the window frame, he made his way, hand over hand, across to the other side. All the while the very, very hungry crocodiles snapped greedily at his heels—but Nick was much to quick for them.

At last he reached the other side and ran toward
the pitch-black forest. His knees were knocking,
so frightened was he; but he wanted to get away
as far as possible from the Nasty Knight.

Soon he was deep inside the woods. When
he was too tired to take another step, he lay
down beneath a bush and immediately fell
fast asleep.

In the middle of the night, someone grabbed him by the shoulder and pulled him up in the air. It wasn't Nestor the Nasty and his guards, but it was just as bad. Five rough-looking robbers bent over him and laughed a blood-curdling robbers' laugh.

"A good catch!" yelled one. "He can chop our wood, fetch our water, feed our animals, and wash our dishes."

The robber chief grinned in delight and showed all his missing teeth. Then he noticed the coin.

"And what's that shining in his hand?" he shouted.

The robber who held Nick shook him so hard that the coin fell to the ground.

"Gold! Real gold!" the robbers shrieked in delight.

"Where did you get that?!" the chief roared.

"From Sir Nestor the Nasty," Nick answered quickly. "And there's a lot more gold where this came from."

"Really?!" The robbers' eyes gleamed greedily. "Then show us the way to his treasure trove, boy."

"Only if you promise me my freedom," said Nick. "And a small purse of gold pieces."

"Agreed!" the robbers growled.

And so they all crept back to the castle and made their
way almost unnoticed across the moat.

The robbers couldn't believe their eyes when they entered the treasure chamber—never in their lives had they seen so much gold. (And that says something . . . .)

"It's all ours!" they cheered.

"And I am free," said Nick.

"Oh no, you're not!" shouted the chief with a mean twinkle in his eyes. "We tricked you! We still need you to chop our wood, fetch our water, do our dishes—and carry our treasure chests."

They laughed their mean laugh and plunged their hands into the piles of gold.

That was the last straw. Nick ran straight past the robbers to the window and was just about to jump out—when the robber chief grabbed him by the collar and shouted, **"OH NO, YOU DON'T!"**

What happened next was even worse. The chief's words echoed loudly through the castle, and in no time at all Sir Nestor and his knights were wide-awake. With their swords in hand, they stormed into the treasure chamber.

"Robbers!" they cried, and a wild battle began.

To draw his sword, the robber chief had to let go of Nick. If only he hadn't!

Quick as a flash, Nick swiped the glowing coin from the chief's hand and leaped out of the window.

"He's got the coin!" yelled the chief. "Catch him!"

"The coin? Surely not my magic coin?!!" bellowed the Nestor the Nasty. "Seize him, knights!"

But because none of his men moved fast enough for Sir Nestor, he squeezed through the window right after the robbers.

There they all dangled from the rope—Sir Nestor the Nasty, the five robbers, and Nick; and then the rope began to groan and creak beneath their weight. Then it groaned and creaked even more. Nick knew what would happen next.

With one last huge leap he jumped to safety. Only then did he realize, that he had accidentally dropped the coin.

Suddenly there was a great RAAAAAAATCH and
a SPLASH,
SPLASH,
SPLASH,
SPLASH,
SPLASH,
SPLASH!

And the Nasty Knight and the robbers tumbled headfirst into the water, where the hungry crocodiles were already waiting for them . . . .

Now things went very fast. What happened next was
quite a big surprise.

The moment the coin hit the water . . .

there was a great hissing sound, . . .

and in a flash Sir Nestor and the five robbers all turned
into crocodiles!

When the people up in the castle saw what had happened, they began to cheer. Without the Nasty Knight, they were once again free! Even the crocodiles in the moat smiled happily. You see they were all lonely lady crocodiles and immediately fell in love with the six new gentlemen.

From that day on, Nick made sure that at last his poor mother and his family had enough to eat every day. And not just them. He also made sure that the crocodiles never went hungry again.

The magical crocodile coin, though, had vanished deep, deep down at the bottom of the murky moat. And if you or anyone else you know hasn't found it, it's probably still there.

First published in the United States, Great Britain, Canada, Australia, and
New Zealand in 2012 by NorthSouth Books Inc., an imprint of NordSüd Verlag AG,
CH-8005 Zürich, Switzerland.

Distributed in the United States by NorthSouth Books Inc., New York 10016.
Library of Congress Cataloging-in-Publication Data is available.
ISBN: 978-0-7358-4091-1
Printed in China by Leo Paper Products Ltd., Heshan, Guangdong, June 2012.
1 3 5 7 9 • 10 8 6 4 2

www.northsouth.com